Tales of Wisdom and Folly

Tales of Wisdom and Folly™

Book One

To Byron
Enjoy the ~~tales~~ tAils! 🐾
Francelle Blum

Francelle Blum

Tiny Lion Publishing
Houston, Texas

Tales of Wisdom and Folly

Copyright © 2013 by Francelle LeNaee Blum

ISBN 978-0-9895583-0-3

For ordering information please contact:

Tiny Lion Publishing
PO Box 271191
Houston, TX 77277

TalesofWisdomandFolly.com

Book Production
Marvin D. Cloud

Illustrations
Francelle LeNaee Blum

Printed in the United States

To the First Star at Night
And the Moon Shining Bright

To old ones and little ones
Who set their sights high

For you, my dear reader
May you find joy inside

. . . and for my mom
&
Nancy NoWorth Shortfellow

™

Contents

Folly Gets a Crooked Tail

I once knew an old woman who lived in a cozy cottage with a big rocking chair and a lovely garden. The old lady had two cats. One was named Wisdom, because he was wise. The other was named Folly, because he was not.

Every day the lady petted her cats. She stroked their chins and told them they were very fine.

"Wisdom, what beautiful eyes have you."

"Folly, such a magnificent tail you sport. Be sure to keep it safe."

Each day the lady would feed her cats. She gave them the very best foods—fish, beef, and chicken.

"Dear Wizzy, how slowly you savor your meal," she would say. "How lovely and plump you've become."

Wisdom would purr and rest on the rug. He was contented and healthy and wise.

"Sweet Folly, slow down. Don't inhale your feast."

But Folly would eat at full speed then dart off to play. He would run and jump and leap. Folly reasoned that food tasted too good to go slow, and life was too short to just lie around and digest. That is . . . until he got sick and lost his meal.

Each day the old lady sat in her chair. Each day she rocked and rocked.

Wisdom watched with his beautiful sage eyes and gauged the rhythm of the chair.
Back and forth.
　　Back and forth.
　　　　Wisdom stayed three feet away.

Folly looked at the chair swaying beautifully to and fro. He could not resist coming close to the fun. Folly sat just inches away.

One day Folly let out a screech. "Yeeeoooowww!"

"I told him once, and I told him twice!" Wisdom moaned to himself. "Now he's gotten too close and rocked a crimp in his tail."

The old woman petted Folly's head and gave him a bandage. But his tail stayed crooked
                    —forever rocking-chair damaged.

The old woman loved her cats very much.
She loved them for who they were—crooked tails and all. And each day without fail, she petted their chins and told them they were very fine.

"Wisdom, what lovely wise eyes you have! How fat and healthy you are!" were things the old woman would say.

"Oh, Folly, what a sweet fellow. Such energy you have! But with that skinny tummy and that crooked tail . . . I should think you would learn!"

You see, Folly still lay too close to the old woman's chair, even after he had broken his tail.

He still ate too fast and got sick at his tummy.

Yes, Folly was lively and full of fun. But he did not listen, and he would not learn.

So, it fell to Wisdom to take care of his friend, to steer Folly from trouble and keep him from harm, and to warn him over and over again:

"Folly!
Get your tail out from under that chair!"

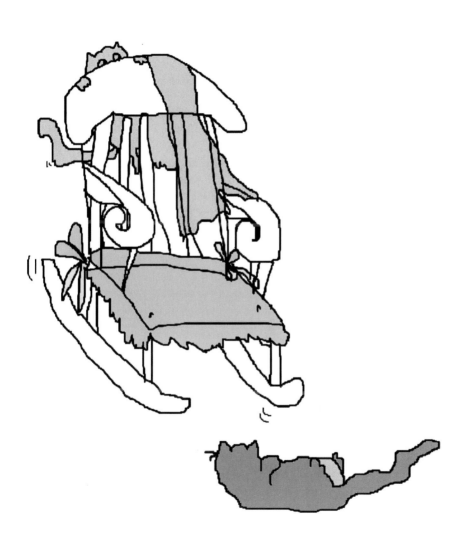

Slithy Loses His Tail

One bright sunny morning, the old woman went into her garden. She had a lovely garden. In it she grew flowers, herbs, and peas.

The old woman held open her screen door and said, "Come, little kitties. But remember to stay safely inside the yard. And, Folly, please remember that eating lizards will make you sick. And, don't forget that bees will sting your nose!"

"Yes! Remember last time!" said Wisdom.

The woman grabbed her basket from its hook and headed for the pea vines.

"These peas look lovely. I think I'll have some for lunch."

She carefully picked the very best and put them in her basket.

Wisdom and Folly were happy to be outdoors.
Cats like warm sunshine and fresh morning air.

Wisdom gently explored the garden. He had outdoor friends who lived there. Slithy was one of them.

Slithy was the garden's biggest lizard. He lay sunning himself on a big round rock.

Wisdom stretched out on the ground next to Slithy's rock. The lizard and the cat smiled at one another, all peaceful and calm. Together they lay quietly, enjoying the sun.

Along came Folly.

Folly saw not a friend in Slithy, but a lizard to be had.
    In an instant, he had pounced.
Why he scared that poor lizard half to death!

Slithy jumped two-feet high in the air.
    Away he ran, with lightning speed!

He ran through the petunias and right through the violets.
Folly chased him. He was right behind!

Slithy ran under the basil bush, but the cat followed still.

Slithy ran harder!
    He ran under the spinach and out the other side.

Folly was right on Slithy's heels—or *tail*, as the case may be!

Up a garlic plant went the lizard, where he suddenly stopped
and said, "Pheeeeew!"

The cat also stopped and wrinkled his nose.
He, too, let out a "Phew!"

"I'll hide in the woman's basket," thought Slithy. "She won't let that cat in there!"

With quick leap, the lizard jumped to the old woman. He landed on her leg and began to climb.
   She squealed!
   She jumped!
        And, yet further he climbed.

Up her leg, and around her tummy.
Over her shoulder and down her arm, and . . .
       Oh, it really was not very funny.

That poor old woman!
She grabbed her chest.
She threw down her basket and shook out her dress!
Out flew the peas!
And the old woman fell to her knees.

The basket with Slithy dropped to the ground. Right into the compost, which smelled and sm-m-melled.

Folly had followed Slithy through it all.
Behind the lizard he'd run.
Up the woman's leg and her tummy all round.
    Then, with a THUMP, he, too, landed on the ground.

Folly was right on top of the basket.
The lizard was trapped inside.

"Yeoww! I've caught a reptile!" Folly said with pride.

But when he looked down, no Slithy could be found. Why, that stealthy lizard had left the basket and hidden in the ground.

Disappointed, Folly looked to the old woman. It was then he saw what he had done.

That poor, sweet lady was lying flat on her back!

Oh, what a mess!

There were peas in her hair and peas in her toes!

Her hair was disheveled, and her glasses sat crooked on her nose.

"Uh oh," thought Folly.

The old woman slowly rose to her feet. The scrape on her knee would need some attention. But then she began to laugh. She laughed at her good fortune, just happy that nothing was broken, not an ankle, a wrist, or even a toe.

"Whew, that was lucky," she said.

Of course, this meant that for lunch she would have no peas.

Wisdom rushed to the scene.

"Look what you've done, Folly! The lizard is nervous, and the woman is fragile. You must be more careful!"

Folly felt bad. He wondered what to do.

"I'll tell you," chirped Wisdom. "Go rub against her ankle. Look sort of sad and meow really sweet. She'll know you are sorry, if you apologize right away."

Folly listened to Wisdom and told the woman he was sorry in that special cat way.

The old woman bent down and petted her cat.

"Oh, Folly, my pet! You must learn to think and not just run wild like that. But what a sweet kitty you are. I know you are sorry, and would never be mean."

The old woman and her cats went back indoors where the lady tended her wounds.

From his hiding place, the lizard peeked out. When Slithy saw that Folly was safe in the house, he rolled over and sighed with relief.

Then he looked down and yelled . . .

"Yikes! That fool cat got my tail!"

The Pantry Fiasco

One day at feeding time, only Wisdom came when the old woman called. "Wizzy, where's our little rambunctious one?" the woman asked.

Wisdom meowed the clearest he could, to tell the woman that Folly was nowhere to be found.

"Where could he be?" she wondered aloud. "It's not like him to miss a meal."

"Here Kitty-kitty-kitty," the woman called.

Wisdom followed the old woman through the house. He mewed loudly for Folly to come.

Together they searched every nook and every cranny. They looked high, and they looked low. They looked in, and they looked out. Where, oh where, was Folly?

Folly was not in the living room or under the dining room chairs. He was not under a bed, in a window, or hiding in the shower. Where could that silly cat be?

Wisdom and the woman began to worry. Why didn't Folly meow or make a noise? Could he be hurt?

The woman put her hands on her hips and tried to think. "Now where have we not looked? What have we skipped?"

"I do not know," thought Wizzy. "But I'll bet Folly has made a mess, wherever he is."

"The pantry. That's it!" said the woman.

Wisdom followed the woman to the pantry closet. That's where she stored her items of bulk—like flour for bread, sugar for cake.

They saw the pantry door was opened part way—just enough room for a cat to slink through. The woman pulled the handle and jerked open the door. At that very moment, they heard a loud cat screech, and a cloud of white powder billowed from inside!

White stuff covered the woman.
It covered the cat.
It covered the kitchen.
It covered all of that!

With a cough and spit, the woman wiped her eyes.

"Flour," she said.

She was completely white from her head to toe. She looked like a snowman wearing a lady's dress.

Wisdom, too, was covered nose to tail.
He looked like . . . well, like a very white cat.

When the flour settled a bit, they could see Folly perched high on a shelf. He sat proudly up there with a mouse in his mouth!

Below him were flour sacks, ripped all to shreds. He'd climbed on them, you see, when he chased that mouse. The paper bags had been no match for Folly's sharp claws.

"Oh, my!" said the old woman.

She took one step forward and felt something crunch under her feet.

"Oh, not the sugar, too!" she cried. "I'll never get this clean."

Wisdom stepped back and shook his head. Now they would all need a bath, and he just hated that.

Folly sat still. He didn't move an inch.

The old woman stood on her tiptoes to coax him down. The mouse lay limp and still between Folly's teeth, just dangling by its tail.

"Here Kitty-kitty. Give me the mouse."

But as she reached up to pull down the cat, the mouse let out a squeak and squiggled to be free!

That poor lady was so startled she fell on her seat.

Wisdom heard sugar grinding underneath. *Crrrrunch.*

"Oh! That hurt," she cried. "That cat will be the death of me yet!"

Folly dropped the mouse, which ran out the door. He thought to pursue, but Wisdom stepped forth.

"Stay put, Folly. Look what you've done!"

"Yes! Look at me! I've saved our pantry from a mouse!"

Wisdom just glared.

Folly purred and rubbed his furry body against the old woman, who was still on the floor, wondering if she could get up.

"Are you proud of me?" he mewed.

"Oh, you naughty kitten. Look at what a mess you've made. I'll be cleaning for days."

Folly mewed some more. He added a purr.
Then—very cutely—he licked flour from her nose.
The old woman laughed and gave him a hug.

"Well, at least nothing's broke," she said. "And I can still walk . . . I hope."

Wisdom shook his body. Then he shook it some more.
"I'll never get all this flour off my paws!"

"But, Wizzy," Folly answered, "at least nothing's broke!

. . . Say, this sugar stuff tastes good!"

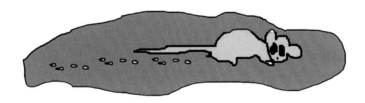

Indoor Deluge

One rainy afternoon the old woman went for a drive. She left Wisdom and Folly alone in the house, where she expected they would be safe and dry.

"Be good, my little pets. I'll bring back treats."

Wisdom and Folly perched in the window. They watched the woman's car drive through the puddles and waited until she waved goodbye from her driver's side window.
"What shall we do?" thought the pair.

Wisdom knew that rainy days were a good time to catch up on one's sleep and to do a little extra grooming. He curled up on the warm rug in front of the sofa and examined his tail.

Wizzy did have a nice tail. He took care to keep it out of harm's way, far from rocking chairs and slamming doors, unlike Folly, who by now had two kinks in his tail.

Wisdom decided to give his tail a good licking. After that, he thought to take a nice long nap.

But Folly was not content to groom or to sleep. He roamed the room, mewing with boredom.
"What to do? What to do? There's nothing to chase. No mice or lizards. What to do?"

Wisdom meowed wise advice. "The old woman will be home soon with treats. Let's be rested and clean so that we can have fun when she comes."

Folly was not in the mood for wise council. He wanted to play. He had lots of energy, and he felt like being silly that day.

Folly roamed through the house, just looking for something to do, something to chase.

Before long, Wisdom heard Folly make a thump. He decided to check on his foolish little friend. No telling what Folly was into.

Wisdom found Folly in the bathroom, just staring at his face in the mirror.

"That's not so bad," thought Wisdom. "He'll be fine."
But he cautioned, "Stay out of trouble. Remember: Think before you do."

"Of course! Don't I always?" Folly mewed.

Then Folly reached out and put his paw on the faucet.

"Now what did I just say? You don't need faucet water. Go drink from your bowl."

But Folly had watched the woman many times. She just turned the knob and water dripped down—just like the rain from the sky. He wanted to do it, too.

Folly pushed with his right paw, and he pushed with his left. But the faucet would not budge. No water came out.

"See there," mewed Wisdom. "The faucet is not for cats. Come with me. We'll take a nap."

Folly thought, and he thought.
　　　　"The sink is fun, but that bathtub . . . "

"Oh, no! Folly don't! Stay away from that tub!"

Folly ignored his friend and jumped right in. He pawed and played with the drain plug. It was fun, you see, because it made noise. He made it go up and go down, until it stuck and locked into place.

With the drain closed tight, that fun was over.

Folly shifted his thoughts to the big faucet above the drain. He jumped on the edge of the tub and bent over to see.

With his right paw he pushed one knob. It did not move.
He pushed with his left paw.
Still the faucet stayed put.

"Oh, please, Folly, please. Come away from that water spout before it is too late! This is foolish. It can be nothing but trouble."

But Folly kept playing, pawing at the knobs until one of them finally turned to the right. Out came the water with a great whooshing sound.

"Oh, Folly. This is not good! Turn it off, turn it off!"

Wizzy's cries were to no avail.

The water was on, the drain was down, the tub was filling, and there was no woman around!

Higher and higher the water flowed.

Folly jumped for joy.

"Just look at the water that I've made. It's better than being outside in the rain!"

Wisdom worried and shook his head. Cats aren't supposed to like water. Didn't Folly know that?

Soon the water filled the tub and began to spill over the top.

Folly and Wisdom went to the door. They watched water spread across the entire floor.

"It's coming our way. That carpet is not supposed to get wet. Oh, Folly, what's next!" cried Wisdom.

The water kept coming . . .

Out the bathroom door it flowed, onto the carpet, and down the hall.

The cats stayed just a few feet ahead.
They climbed the stairs and watched from above.
It was a virtual flood.
No. It was a real flood!

Just then the cats heard keys rattling at the door.
The woman was home! They were saved!

From their perch on the stairs, the cats watched the woman put down her umbrella and say, "How nice it is to come into my dry house."

Then squish went her shoes, and she looked about. It was then that she saw the indoor deluge—that means *a lot of water!*

She noticed the water was coming from the bathroom. "Surely, I didn't leave water running," she thought. "I'm not that forgetful."

She hurried to the tub and shut off the faucet. She quickly bent over to pull the drain, when . . . oops, the woman slipped on the wet floor!

Wisdom screeched, "Be care—eow—ful!"

"Ouch! I can't believe I just fell!"

She looked herself over to see if all was O.K.

"I'll have a bruise," she said, "but nothing's broke!"

Wisdom gave Folly an unhappy look. "See what's happened!"

The woman called the neighbor, and she called the carpet cleaner.

"Yes, I fell down, but I'm alright," she told them.
"It was my own fault, you see. I left the water running. I can't blame sweet little Folly this time."

The neighbor was glad the lady had not broken a leg, or an arm, or a hip. He helped her clean the mess and gave her a cup of warm honey and milk.

"Those poor little cats," he said, "just trapped on the stairs like that. They must have been so scared."

"Oh, I know," said the woman.

Wisdom was not pleased with Folly that day!

"Folly, you unwise feline. The carpet's a mess, and the woman's backside is blue! This is what happens when you don't listen."

Folly said, "Well, at least nothing's broke! . . . Hey, where do you think she put the treats?"

For that, Wizzy swatted Folly on his head and gave him a stern hiss.

The old woman saw this and said, "I just don't know what gets into Wizzy sometimes."

Birthday Blowout

Day 1—A Blustery Start

One breezy spring morning, the old woman said it was going to be a busy day. She had much to do.

"Why, there is too much to remember," she said. "I need a list."

Wisdom and Folly listened to the old woman as she jotted down her chores. There were gardening tasks and kitchen work, too.

"Oh my, but it is a blustery day—just like it was for that bear," she said. "I hope it doesn't mess up my hair!"

The woman giggled at her own rhyme.

"What bear?" wondered Folly.

"I don't know," said Wisdom.

Then the woman laughed out loud and declared,
"I'm a poet and didn't know it.
But my feet show it.
They are Longfellows!"

Wisdom nudged Folly and smiled, as the woman tied her shoes.

"What's up with her?" Folly mewed.

"Oh, she is just in a very good mood," smiled Wisdom. "I guess she likes windy days."

Folly wanted to know what long feet had to do with poetry.

"I have no idea," said Wisdom.

The woman put down her list, popped a hat on her head, and bounded out the door.

"Meeeewwwwww, Meeewww," cried the cats. She had forgotten and left them inside.

"Oh, I'm sorry fellows. Did you want to come, too?"

The old woman opened the kitchen door. "I guess I should have put you on the list to remember, huh?"

"Oh, I'm so excited!" she said.

"Meeee, toooo!" howled Folly as he bolted out the door.

Wisdom lingered a moment, sniffing the air and looking about. He never rushed out. It just wasn't wise.

"Come on, Wizzy. Hurry now. I have much to do. Much to do!" said the woman.

The old woman tightened her cap and braced herself to stand tall. The wind was so strong that she had trouble walking.

"Look, my fur's all askew!" chirped Folly as he bounced behind. His hair was blowing wild.

"Askew? Now where did he learn that word?" Wisdom wondered.

The old woman went to the storage shed. She pulled out one patio table and many folding chairs. They were covered in dust and needed to be cleaned. The old woman set to work with a rag and bucket of water.

"Oh, these really need to be repainted," said she. "But I'm afraid there is only time for a cleaning."

"In time for what?" Folly asked Wisdom. "Has she said?"

"No. She hasn't mentioned," Wizzy replied. "But the last time she got out those chairs and was this happy, we had a party."

"A party?" asked Folly. "What's that?"

"It is when other humans come and do fun things together. Sometimes they play games. Sometimes they give gifts. But mostly they eat."

"Don't they eat at their homes?" Folly inquired.

"They eat treats, special human treats. Nothing you would like—cakes, cookies, and something called nachos."

Wisdom and Folly lay behind a box to hide from the wind. From there, they watched as the woman worked to clean and improve the state of her chairs.

One chair blew over twice. The washcloth flew away and had to be chased. And a sudden gust sent soap suds right into the woman's face.

"And this makes our woman happy?" Folly asked as he watched her spit out bubbles.

"Yes. It works like this: Something special happens—like a birthday or a wedding. This makes people want to eat. The people all get together and eat special treats in one place. They call it celebrating.

"The old woman fusses about for two days, making the house and yard look pretty. She cleans, decorates, and cooks, and worries about her hair.

"The people come. They eat the treats, laugh, and talk.

"Then they leave, and she cleans up the mess."

Folly was confused because usually the old woman was not in the mood to clean up messes.

"What do we do, Wizzy? Do we get to help?"

"Oh, no! No. Indeed, not. We stay out of the way." Wisdom was firm.

"But . . ." Folly tried to protest. A party sounded exciting.

"Now, listen, Folls. . . . " Wisdom was very serious.

"This is what cats do at parties. If the party is outdoors, we can observe the humans from under the shrubs over there. If the party is indoors, and if we feel brave, we can watch them from the top of the stairs. But usually the best plan is to hide in the closet and take a nap."

"What? Why?" Folly mewed. "Don't we want to have fun, too?"

"No. It is not safe. The people are nice, you see. They mean well. But humans are clumsy folk. Not graceful like cats. They will step on your tail and never even look down!"

Wizzy thought for a minute and added more advice.

"Especially, if there is music. If you hear music and someone says the word *dance*—Run away! Get to high ground. You don't want to be underfoot when the dancing happens. Clumsy, I tell you."

Folly began to think that Wisdom was a bit overly concerned.

The old woman finished cleaning the chairs. The wind was too strong to leave them outside.

"I'll put these in the garden room," she said.

The garden room had tall windows and was full of light. A party there would be just the thing, she decided. Outdoors was too windy, and tomorrow's forecast was for more of the same.

As the woman made decorating decisions, the wind blew open the garden room door. In fact, it blew open once, twice, and then once more. Twice it almost popped Folly in the face.

"I had better put a latch on that door to keep it closed," said the woman.

"There. That should keep it," she said when she was done. "We can't have the wind coming inside.

"Now come along, kitties. There's more to do and very little time. I hope I get it all done."

Folly was sure the woman needed help. Why, she fretted and fussed all the day—getting just the right table cloths and napkins, and baking a cake.

But Wisdom wisely kept Folly out of the way.

At the end of the day, the woman looked at her work. She was pleased with what she had done.

Bright colored plates sat ready for food. The chairs were decorated with bows and balloons. Paper flowers in vases made the room look cheery. And a festive banner hung over the door. It read: *FELIZ CUMPLEAÑOS*.

"Yes," she thought, "the garden room is a good place. The party will be grand!"

With windows for walls, the cheery sun came in, but the troublesome wind stayed out.

"It is just perfect," she declared.

"Well, little kitties, what sweet cats you are. Thank you for being patient all day!"

She stroked her cats' chins and told them they were fine.

"What good boys you have been! Now let's all get a good night's sleep."

Wisdom was glad Folly had listened. Thank goodness he had acted wisely—and not acted out!

Miracles never cease. Wisdom could only hope that Folly would be good tomorrow, too.

But could he hold out two days in a row?

Day 2—Party Time!

Tomorrow soon came. It was time for the party!

The old woman put on a bright striped dress and huge hat. "Oh, I do like this sombrero," she said to the mirror.

Wisdom showed Folly the special human treats.
"Look at the food, and you'll know what kind of party it is."

This was a birthday party. You could tell because of the little wax sticks stuck into the cake. Wizzy explained that the people would gather around the cake, set fire to these sticks, and sing a song.

"What?" screeched Folly. "We aren't supposed to play with fire!"

"I know," said Wisdom. "They do this thing to make the birthday person feel happy."

Folly still thought this sounded odd. Even he could see it was unwise.

"Yes, my little buddy, it can be dangerous. But the woman is very, very careful. Only wise, grown-up humans are allowed to light the little sticks. The birthday person blows them out right away."

Wisdom was pleased with Folly for thinking about safety and remembering rules.

"Folly, my friend, you've been very wise this week. I am proud of you."

"Thank yeeeewww," Folly mewed.

Wisdom and Folly agreed that people do some very strange things. The two cats took a place on the stairs and waited to see what would happen.

Soon the doorbell began to ring. With each ring, the old woman welcomed another guest. The guests wore funny colored hats that matched the table decorations.

"How did they know to do that?" Folly wondered.

Wisdom didn't know.

The woman turned on the music machine, and people began to sing. They sang silly songs that made them laugh. They ate nachos and cookies and drank something pink.

Then the old woman and a handsome young man put paper flowers in their mouths and danced dramatically across the floor. Everyone laughed, creating a big roar!

Someone yelled, "Olé!"

The cats did not know why the people did these things, but it was fun to watch just the same.

Then the big event happened. The old woman pranced out, holding the birthday cake high above her head. She put it in front of a very old man they all called Uncle Joe.

He said, "Well, I had better enjoy this. I might not have many more!"

The people all laughed and said he would live to be one-hundred-and-four!

"This is where they sing and light the fire," Wisdom told Folly. "It always makes me nervous."

The woman took out a tiny torch and began to light candles.
One, two, three . . . six, seven . . . *Wow!*
There were a lot of candles! So many that they lost count. Soon, the whole cake was alight. The people marveled and "ooh-ed" at this sight.

"I've never seen one that bright," worried Wisdom.
He laid down his ears and tucked his tail in tight.

Uncle Joe said he would need help. There were too many candles for his weak breath.
"I don't think I have enough wind for all that," he said.

Folly was confused. He thought a serious problem had occurred. The old man needed help!
He needed wind!

Folly rushed to the rescue. Across the room he ran!

He ran so fast no one saw as he passed by.
Onto a guest table he climbed!
If only he could reach the latch. Could he jump that high?

With all his might, Folly made one huge leap. He soared high in the air, his front paw aimed for the latch that held shut the door. Then with one swift swat, the latch popped!

Folly fell to the ground, and the door blew open with a bang! A huge gust of wind surged through the room.

Candles blew out, and hats blew off.
Flower vases fell to the floor.

"Oh, my skirt!" squealed a girl.

"Oh, my hair!" cried another.

The wind was so strong it blew an empty chair on its side. It even blew a candle into Uncle Joe's ear!

"What happened? What happened?" people were saying. "Quick! Close the door!"

When it was all over and the people calmed down, Uncle Joe looked at the cake that had spilled in his lap. The cake began to wiggle.

"Look! The cake's grown a tail!" someone cried. "A crooked tail!

"Oh, my," said the old woman.

"Uh oh," mewed Wizzy.

"Meow," said the cake.

Uncle Joe started laughing and shaking all over. He laughed so hard he almost fell out of his seat!

"Why, this is the best birthday party I have ever had! That cat of yours really knows how to blow out the cake!"

"Are you sure you're alright?" the woman asked Joe.

"Yes, I'm fine."

"You're sure nothing's broke?"

"No, not a thing!—I love birthdays. And, I love cats!"

The Great Dye Spill

Wisdom and Folly sat at the edge of the table, admiring a large basket of eggs. There were many eggs. They were very white and pretty.

The cats wondered why the old woman had so many eggs. Each morning, you see, the woman cooked one for breakfast. And sometimes she put eggs in other things like cookie dough or pancake batter. But she never used more than one or two. No more than four, to be sure.

What on earth could she need with all those eggs?

"Careful now, kitties." The old woman petted Wisdom behind the ears.

"Don't break my eggs," said she, as she stroked Folly's chin.

The cats then heard a song coming from the woman's apron pocket. She pulled out a little box and said, "Hello."

The cats always thought it strange that the woman talked to the little box. It seemed even stranger that the box talked back. Cats, you see, don't bother with phones.

"Oh, yes. The eggs are wonderful, Mary. Your chickens lay the very best!" said the woman. "Yes, yes. Better than Juan's."

Some squeaks came from the box, and the old woman answered them.

"Yes, I will. I will color them with my homemade dye. They will be beautiful. Not to worry."

Another pause, then the woman said, "That's true. The boys and girls do like hunting the beautiful eggs."

Then she told the box "Thank you" but declined its offer to help. Barney the postman's grandson was coming to help with the eggs.

Folly's ears perked up. He loved having company! How fun!

Wizzy's ears went down a bit as he contemplated the news. He enjoyed company, too. But Folly was prone to silliness when company came. Trouble might ensue.

"Now I know what these eggs are all about," Wizzy mewed.

Wisdom told Folly about Easter. This is a time when the old woman makes the eggs look pretty. Then she and other grownups hide the eggs for children to find.

The children wear pretty clothes and look for the pretty eggs in the grass. They look under trees and behind boxes. Sometimes they even look under cats! It makes them happy to find the eggs.

"Sounds grand!" Folly meowed. "I like to hunt things, too. Especially lizards. I love hunting lizards!"

"Yes, I know!" scolded Wizzy. "That is precisely why Slithy wants to move next door!"

The doorbell rang. "I'm here to help, Ma'am," said a boy.

"Welcome, young man. Come on in," the woman said with joy.

The boy had met the cats once before. They liked the boy, and he liked them. His name was Jim.

"It looks like Folly's been in trouble again!" said Jim.

"Oh, my!" said the woman. "I had not seen that bubble gum in his fur."

She took some scissors and cut out the goo.

Gently she scolded, "Shame on you."

The old woman set about boiling the first batch of eggs. They had to cook and cool before they could be dyed. She placed them in a pot of water. Then she turned on the heat. She poured on some salt, a whole big bunch.

Before long the water boiled hot. Jimmy and the cats heard the eggs begin to rattle. They were curious and wanted to watch.

But the old woman gave Jim another job to do. He and the cats were to stay across the room, she said. The cooking part is for grownups. It is not safe for animals or little boys.

Jim's job was to sort the uncooked eggs by size. The woman asked him to group them into three baskets.

"This basket is for the regular medium eggs—like this one," she said. "If they are really big, put them in this one. And here's one to hold the smallest eggs—like these puny little things over here."

The woman smiled and put a label on each:
Small, *Medium*, and *Really Big*.

She winked and leaned in close. "But don't tell that Mary I said that," she said. "She doesn't think her hens could possibly lay puny eggs."

With a laugh and wink, she left the boy to his task. Jim loved to spend time at this house, with such easy laughter and two cats, to boot.

Jim did a good job, thoughtfully sorting and carefully placing the eggs in just the right basket. Sometimes he would change his mind and move a medium egg to the puny basket, or the other way around.

When he finished, he went to the refrigerator and helped himself to some juice. But the boy had overlooked just one egg. He had left it lying on the flat table.

Wisdom saw the situation and knew that with Folly around this was a formula for disaster.

"Folly," he said. "Let's lie very still on the floor. I think the eggs might break if we were to jiggle the table."

But Folly was not good at being still. And he wanted very much to touch the egg. It was so smooth and so white, wobbling about.

What a temptation! It was too much to resist.

So, when Wizzy closed his eyes to rest, Folly sneaked onto the table. Slowly, he crept toward the egg. Gently, he touched it with his paw. It felt smooth and cool.

He touched it again. It bobbled a bit, and Folly liked that.

Folly again used his paw and gave it a light swat. The egg bobbled some more and kind of rolled to the side.

"How fun!" thought Folly. "A play ball!" Folly swatted once more.

The egg rolled hard, and it rolled fast! Off the table it went with a Ka Plop and a *Splat!*

"Uh oh!" said the boy. "Folly's broken an egg!"

"Uh oh, is right!" Wizzy thought.
Then loudly he mewed, "For pity's sake, Folly, get your paw out of that mess!"

The old woman shooed Folly away.

"Oh well," she said, "at least it was just an egg that fell. It could have been me . . . and the egg is much easier to pick up off the floor than I would be!"

Jim laughed hard at that. "Let me do that for you. I'll clean it up. Just tell me what to do."

The cats watched from the corner of the room. "I told you so!" Wisdom told his friend. "Eggs are not toys, they are food!"

"Hey, this tastes pretty good," said Folly as he licked raw egg from his paw.

Wisdom just sighed. He hoped this one little mess was the only trouble Folly would cause.

Soon the woman and boy were ready to dye the boiled eggs. Together they arranged small bowls on the table. They poured special water called dye into each. One was blue, one was red. Another was yellow. There was even a bowl of purple.

Wisdom saw the beautiful colors sparkling and splashing about.

"Come on, Folls," he advised. "Let's take a nap . . . in the other room."

But Folly wanted to watch the pretty bowls. He wanted to see the eggs change colors.

"How did you get the wonderful colors?" Jim asked.

"Oh, I have a list of things from my garden that will make the colors. Let me show you," the woman responded.

She did this, she said, by putting different foods and flowers into water and vinegar. The color depended on which food or flower she used.

"Red beets make light red and pink, which makes sense. Blueberries make a kind of blue-gray, of course. That is to be expected. And, if you want yellow, use orange peels or golden flowers. That's all simple enough."

Jim nodded.

"But it is not always as you might think," she added with an air of mystery. "There are some colors that seem to emerge like magick from the most unexpected sources. For instance, this lovely light green comes from . . . guess what?"

"Spinach!" said Jim.

"No. This bowl of green dye comes . . . from . . . the skin of six red onions! Yes, that's right. Red onions. Imagine that!"

Jim's eyes opened wide in surprise.
The woman laughed heartily. The boy laughed, too.

"But don't drink it," she joked. "Or your breath will smell like . . . Phewww Wee!"

The woman pinched her nose when she said this. And Jim did it, too. "Phewww Wee!"

"And, your mouth will turn green! That's even worse!" she went on.

"A stinky green mouth!" said Jim.

They laughed, and they laughed. The cats purred, too.

"It is sort of like magick," said the boy, "getting green color from something red!"

Folly thought so, too. And Wisdom mewed that he agreed.

"What other tricks do you know?" Jim asked with a smile. "Can you tell my fortune?"

"Oh, that requires tea leaves and will take extra time. Let's save that for Halloween."

While the boy and woman were laughing and having fun, Folly grew curious about that bowl of green Easter-egg dye. He sneaked to the table, and he took a sniff. It smelled like vinegar and onions—phew, was right—but he didn't care. Cats are like that, you know. Folly stuck his paw right into the bowl!

"Oh no!" Wizzy meowed, using his most urgent cat sounds. "Stop him!" he cried.

The woman and the boy turned to see why Wizzy was upset. The cat pointed his nose in Folly's direction. But they were too slow, and Folly too fast. His paw had been dunked, dunked in deep and jerked out fast. Folly's paw was a dripping green mess.

The old woman screamed and that gave Folly a start. Jim rushed forward, and that made him dart—dart right off the table!

Off he went with a bounding crash. The table rocked, and the bowls did too. Over they went, spilling the beautiful colors all over the place.

Blue flowed in one direction and dripped on the floor. Tiny drops of orange speckled two chairs and a door.

But the worst of it all was what happened to the green. That bowl landed upside down. You'll never guess where!
              —Right smack on top of Wisdom's head!

Wizzy sat very still. He didn't dare move. Green liquid oozed down his ears and over his nose.

The boy and woman dabbed him with towels. Then they set about cleaning the big, huge, enormous, rainbow-colored mess!

Wisdom wondered to himself where Folly had gone. But Folly was nowhere to be found.

"Just wait until I get my paws on that foolish feline," mewed Wizzy. "If only—just once—he would listen to me!"

"I know how to find him!" Jim said. "I see green paw tracks. Just follow them."

Sure enough, Folly was at the end of the green trail. He had hidden himself, and he had hidden well. He was crouched deep inside an empty trash can.

Folly looked up with big scared eyes. He was frightened by all the noise and commotion. Everyone seemed upset, and he thought it might be his fault.

But Folly was so cute with his wide-eyes and green paws that no one could be mad—not even Wizzy.

The old woman lifted her cat, "Are you all right, Folly?"

She gave him a hug. She scratched his chin. She rubbed his tummy.

"My poor frightened kitty," she said. "Don't be afraid."

Jim chimed in. "Don't worry, Folly. It could have been worse."

"Yes. After all, nothing was broken. No broken bowls. And no broken *bones!* That's all I care about."

The woman laughed at her own words. Jim laughed, too.

Folly felt better. He remembered how Wisdom had taught him to say "I'm sorry."

He rubbed his head against the woman's arm. He looked up with big sweet eyes and purred really cute.

"Oh, Sweetie. I love you, too," she said. "It's O.K. I know you didn't mean to be bad. But you should make amends with Wisdom. Look what you've done to his head."

Folly looked over and saw what had happened.

"Wizzy! What happened? Do you know your head is green?"

Folly thought it was very funny. "You look like a big, furry, green Easter egg!—With a tail!"

Wisdom tried to be patient. "Yes, Folly. You spilled dye on my head. I don't like being green. Cats are not supposed to look silly."

"I'm sorry," said Folly, which made Wisdom feel better. But then the foolish young kitty just had to add, "You know, Wiz, you really should be more careful and learn to stay out of the way."

Reowwwwwwwwwww! Out the door they ran, with Wisdom close on Folly's tail.

"Those are some cats, you have," said Jim.

"Yes, they are," the woman agreed.

"Now what will we do with all these eggs? There is no more dye."

"How about we color them with crayons," she suggested.

"That's an excellent idea!" said Jim. "Hand me a green one, please. I want to make one that looks like Wisdom."

Feathers in the Ice Cream

The old woman kept fresh lemonade in the fridge. Today she added some cherries and crushed the ice to make it extra special. She thought her young friend would be stopping in. He liked to visit and play with the cats.

Wisdom lay sleeping under the kitchen table. Folly perched in the window, trying to spot lizards. Suddenly Folly mewed with excitement and woke up Wizzy.

"It's Jimmy!"

The old woman turned and smiled. She seemed to know what the young cat had said.

"Hello there, young man!" the woman said and handed Jim a glass of cherry-lemonade.

"Mew. Mew. Mew," went Folly as he rubbed his neck on Jim's shoes.

"Folly loves to see you come through that door," the woman told Jim.

"Good to see you, too, Folls," Jim said. "Come here, Wisdom. Don't you want to be petted?"

Wisdom purred and let Jim scratch him behind his ears. Jim was a good boy—even if Folly did get a little out control when Jim came to visit.

Folly began to hop up and down. He ran to the living room and brought back a tiny piece of crumpled up plastic and laid it at Jim's feet.

"That's his favorite new toy," the woman said. "He got it out of the recycling bin."

Jim took the plastic and tossed it high. Folly leaped and caught it midair. He brought it to Jimmy's feet once more.

"Yes, that's right. He plays catch. He'll play that for hours if you are willing to keep throwing it."

The woman and Jim marveled at how high Folly could jump. They were amazed at how he twisted in the air. Wisdom was less impressed. He'd done the same when he was young.

"Are you going to the Fourth of July parade?" asked Jim.

"Yes! Yes! Yes!" purred Folly, as he pawed at Jim's knees.

"No, I think not," said the woman. "I have to get things ready for the picnic here at the house."

"What are we going to eat at the picnic?" Jim wanted to know.

"Lizards! Lizards!" Folly chirped in that silly cat way.

"I think Folly wants you to throw that toy again," said the woman.

"Well, let's see. What is on the menu?" she pondered. "Mary is bringing deviled eggs and egg salad, maybe an egg custard, if she has time. Your family is bringing fried chicken."

"My mom makes wonderful fried chicken!"

"Yes, she does!" the old woman agreed.

"What else will there be?"

"Well, the Gonzales twins promised to bring tuna sandwiches. You know Mary won't eat chicken, so we needed another choice of meat."

"Miss Mary sure loves chickens, doesn't she?" the boy observed.

"Yes. She certainly does."

The old woman told Jim that she planned to serve his favorite lemonade. That's why she was trying out a new flavor each time he came to visit. She would also make homemade ice cream. She might ask his help for that.

The cats perked up in unison and looked at one another. Even Wisdom could get excited about homemade ice cream.

The woman talked about the heat. The trees would give nice shade, she was sure. But perhaps she should put up an outdoor fan to keep her guests cool?

"I want an outdoor fan! I want an outdoor fan!" purred Folly. Jim reached down and tossed his plastic toy in the air.

"Maybe not," Jim told the woman. "Remember all the wind problems on Uncle Joe's birthday?"

"Well, that's true. Maybe we don't want any extra wind coming through."

Wisdom meowed that he agreed. Best to keep things simple.

"How do you make homemade ice cream?" Jim wanted to know.

"Well, if you want to help, let's start with a trip to the store."

So, off went the old woman with Jim in tow. They took a grocery list and a rolling cart. Soon they would be back with cream, eggs, and sugar, bags of ice and boxes of special ice cream salt.

That afternoon, the fun began. The woman told Jim all the secrets she knew about making ice cream.

She had made almost every kind imaginable. She had made many chocolate flavors, all brown and smooth. She had made fruity ice cream, with peaches and strawberries, and some with nuts and macaroon cookies. She had made green, pink, and blue ice cream. Why, in her day, she had done it all!

"Which is the best?" Jim wanted to know.

"Vanilla! Vanilla!" mewed Folly. Jim threw the plastic again.

"Ummmm," purred Wisdom. "Dulce de Leche." He went to sleep dreaming of days gone by when he had licked the bowl clean. Good times.

"Well it depends," the woman answered Jim. "I find that most people like vanilla best. I know you like chocolate. But my favorite is rosemary-pistachio. It is very exotic."

The woman and Jim worked all afternoon. They made several batches before they were through.

The cats stayed close by. Wisdom cautioned Folly a time or two. But mostly he daydreamed about Dulce de Leche.

They labeled the buckets and put them in the freezer. They sampled the flavors, until they ruined their supper. Even Wisdom and Folly got a bowl to lick.

That night everyone went to bed with a full tummy and dreamy thoughts of . . . Vanilla. Chocolate. Rosemary-pistachio. . . . *Dulche de Leche!*

Day 2—Picnic!

About noon the next day, Jim came bounding in the kitchen door!

"I'm here to help!" he declared. The old woman put him to work setting out the napkins and arranging ice cream bowls.

He was full of excitement about that morning's parade. He'd ridden on the Postmaster's float with his Grandpa Barney. It looked like a mailbox. Grandpa Barney drove, while Jim tossed candy to the crowd.

"What's that all about?" Folly inquired.

Wisdom didn't know what a float was or why it had excess candy that needed to be tossed out.

Jim's excitement was contagious. The old woman laughed at his stories, the cats purred. Even Slithy the garden lizard crawled out to listen.

The picnic guests began to arrive. They came in two, threes, and fours. They wore shorts, tennis shoes, and lots of red, white, and blue. Everyone was happy and immediately began to have fun.

"Will we have hamburgers?" asked a hungry teenage boy. "Hot dogs?"

The woman took him aside and said in a whisper, "Oh, no. Mary just got a baby calf. She thinks it is a pet. Please don't mention anything about beef around her. The fried chicken might be too much for her, as it is."

The cats were confused. Fish, beef, and chicken were what they loved best. Except milk. And cream. And tuna, of course.

Folly obeyed Wisdom and was good that day. He stayed close by and out from under human feet. Wisdom was proud of Folly's behavior. He was growing up nicely, all said and done. The two cats sat quietly on a ledge, watching the people mill around. It was a beautiful day.

More guests arrived, and the food table began to fill. The tuna sandwiches and fried chicken were there. There were beans and potato salad, chips and dips. The cherry lemonade that Jim had chosen looked beautiful in a giant glass urn.

But where was Mary? They were waiting on her.

Wisdom cautioned Folly to be patient. The ice cream eating would be after the tuna and chicken. The best way to get a sample was to linger quietly around and look hungry.

"Purr and rub on someone's ankle," Wisdom advised. "When they are finished, they'll put their bowl on the ground. Don't act too eager, though. Let them pet you as you eat. That's how you tell them thank you."

Just when folks began to worry about Mary, she came through the gate, announcing the arrival of deviled eggs and sandwiches.

"Sorry, I'm late. I had trouble with my car. Feathers got stuck in the engine and . . . "

Juggling her bags and boxes of food, Mary walked past Wisdom and Folly. Suddenly, out of the blue—to everyone's surprise—a cocky Rhode Island Red came strutting behind!

"Mee Ow!" Folly jumped straight in air. Wisdom did, too. It was the biggest bird either of them had ever seen.

"It's an eagle!" said Wisdom. "Run for your life!"

"I'll save us, Wizzy!" Folly jumped behind the chicken and gave chase.

The hen clucked, feathers flew. Up, down, and round, went the cat and the bird.

Mary and her deviled eggs went down. Her feet went up and so did her skirt.

"Aggie!" she cried. "Don't let that cat kill my Agnes!"

Aggie and Folly went around empty chairs, over picnic tables, and through a little girl's legs. Onto the porch and back to the yard again—hen and cat, feathers and fur, cackle and scream.

Women yelled!
Children squealed!
Two men took off their caps and sat down for a laugh.

"Save the food!" cried the woman.

Jim rushed to help. He stood guard around the beans and fried chicken.

But you won't believe where that hen ran next! She ran right to the ice cream table!

There on the table were three fresh gallons—chocolate, strawberry, and pistachio-rosemary.

Everyone could see what was about to happen, but no one was fast enough. No one could save the ice cream table.

Up the hen leaped! Her feathers went everywhere.

She landed right in the bucket of strawberry.
That slowed her down, and Folly almost had her!

Just in time, she freed herself from the pink mush. Over the side she flew. The strawberry toppled! The chocolate got smashed!

Off went Aggie!
　　She ran.
　　　　She flew.
　　　　　　She hopped.

To the garden shed she flew, looking for her coop. There she perched on a high rafter, where she squawked and squealed!

Folly was sitting on the ground, when in came the woman, Jim, and the crowd. The woman scooped up her cat. Pistachio-rosemary and feathers stuck to her blouse.

Mary yelled that the cat was awful. Just horrid, he was! How dare he chase her dear little Aggie like that? And, look at the mess, she pointed out.

The woman held Folly close to her chest. His heart was racing, and so was her's.

"There, there, Folls," she whispered. "It's all O.K."

Jim and Wisdom were by her side. Everyone was rattled, and feathers still floated down. Each time the hen squawked, the people jumped.

Mary was livid. She was fit to be tied. "You should get rid of that awful feline!"

"Now, just a minute, my chicken-loving friend! Folly is my pet, and he is a grand pet at that. Around here, cats come first."

"But Aggie is my prime layer. Now she's been traumatized and may never lay another egg!"

"Well, she should have stayed home. I certainly don't remember inviting a hen!—And, you know that I have cats!"

"Oh, my poor Aggie," Mary went on.

About that time, from high on the rafter, the hen let out a loud cackle.
Then *splat*, a very fresh egg dropped onto Mary's head.

"I think she's cured!" someone yelled out. Everyone laughed—even Mary chuckled a bit.

"I'm proud of my cat," said the woman. "He did what good cats do. He chased a bird. And, he chased a really big bird. He's very courageous. Like a tiny lion, he is!"

"Yes, I can see you love that cat. And he is awfully cute," said Mary. "I'm sorry I was angry. But I love my Aggie, too. She must have sneaked in the car when I left. I had no idea she was there."

Everyone agreed that it would be best if Aggie was locked safely in the shed and Folly taken inside to rest.

There was still plenty of ice cream in the freezer, and the food was all fine. The day was not lost. No one was hurt, and nothing had been broken. Well, except for that egg on Mary's head.

When it was all said and done, Wisdom had to tell Folly the truth. He wanted to scold him and tell him to be more cautious. But the truth was that Wisdom was proud of his friend. What a brave young cat, Folly had been!

Halloween Cats & Magickal Hats

Part 1—Witches in the Closet

It was October. Her favorite time of year. The old woman stood on her tiptoes and looked for a distinctive orange storage bin.

"It should be on one of those shelves," she said aloud.

She stepped back and stretched a little taller. She spotted the orange box on the top shelf and read the word HALLOWEEN printed on its side.

"Yes, that's the one," she thought. "Maybe I can pull it down."

But the box was far too high. She tiptoed again and reached as far as she could. It was no use. She could barely touch the ledge.

She chuckled and said, "I must be shrinking in my old age."

The two cats standing at her feet looked at each other. *Shrinking?* they wondered. It didn't sound like a good thing.

"Oh, well," she mumbled. "Now let me think how best to do this without causing bodily injury."

The cats sat down and watched the old woman think. Thinking looked strenuous. Sometimes it took a while.

The woman crossed her arms and tapped her forehead. That helped.

"Well, fellows," she announced, "I could be lazy and just stand on that chair. But I think I'll get the stepladder instead. I'm not as graceful as I used to be."

The older and wiser of the cats nodded his head and meowed his approval. Wisdom liked for the old woman to be cautious. In fact, he like for everyone to be cautious. If only everyone would just be more careful!

The old woman smiled and bent over to stroke Wisdom's head. Then she scurried out the door.

The cats waited.

A few minutes later, she blundered back into the room, awkwardly dragging a small stepladder.

"Watch out, boys!" she warned. "Momma and her Sturdy Two-Stepper coming through!"

She giggled at her words. Then with a determined shove, she plopped the noisy metal contraption onto the floor.

Wisdom scurried off to the side, making sure to give plenty of room. He pulled in his paws and tucked his tail, making himself as small a target as possible. He thought that was best whenever the woman started hoisting heavy objects around.

"Shoo, Folls! You're still in the way," said the woman.

Folly jumped in place, his purring-motor on full speed. His crooked tail pointed straight up in the air. Well, sort of straight up. It was really more like a general meandering skyward, but nonetheless . . . Folly sensed adventure!

"Give me room, silly boy, or we might both take a tumble. Go on over there with Wizzy where it's safe."

Wisdom mewed for Folly to come out of the woman's way. "You might cause her to fall," he warned.

"Good kitties," said the woman as she stepped onto the stool. With one hand she held to the wall. With the other she reached as high as she could.

"Now if I can just . . . get . . . this box down," she groaned.

With a tilt and juggle, she tugged at the box. It made an annoying scraping sound as she pulled it closer to the edge.

The cats lowered their ears.

The box was heavier than the woman remembered, and it was wedged in tight. She managed to scoot it halfway off the shelf.

Then by some miracle, or fate, she pulled the box onto the top of her head. Once that happened, there was no turning back. She had to take it down.

"Down the ladder," she thought. "Backwards down the ladder. Holding this box on top of my head!"

"Lordy, I hope I don't break my neck!" she said to herself.

"Oh, well," she sighed. "Here goes!"

The woman lowered her foot. Her back swayed.

Wisdom saw trouble coming. He remained at a safe distance.

Folly thought it was all good entertainment. He drew closer to get a better view.

"Oooooh," said the woman as the box swayed toward her right arm.

"Yikes," whispered Wisdom, as the box swayed back to her left.

To the right . . . to the left . . . right, right, right . . .
Whoa! . . . back left again.

"Wheee Heee!" purred Folly, as he jumped twice in the air. "I want to ride!"

Finally the woman put her foot back on the step and steadied the box . . . just barely.

With a deep breath, she tried again. Slowly, very slowly, her foot reached downward, feeling for the next step. There it was. One foot in place. Now the next . . .

Folly was wide-eyed. This was thrilling!

Wisdom called to Folly to get out of the closet.
"Hush that and come over here! Give her more room."

But Folly paid no heed. He just fluffed out his crooked tail and gave it a good wiggle.

"Oooh," moaned the woman, as she began to teeter.

"Folly! Come away! Get back!" cried Wisdom.

The woman regained her balance once more and touched one foot to the floor. She was almost—*just almost*—down from the Sturdy Two-Stepper.
She took a deep breath and assessed her situation.

"Just one more step. I've just about made it."

Folly was still at the bottom of the ladder, mewing constantly to show his support.
Then he decided—at just the wrong moment, of course—that a lick on her ankle was just what the old woman needed.

As soon as she felt that wet, scratchy cat-kiss, her whole body jerked, and she let out a yell.
"What was that!"

That scared Folly, and he jumped, too! He jumped through the woman's legs, and right through Sturdy-Steps, Numbers One and Two.

"Oh–oh–oh," she sang out.

The ladder teetered.
The box began to tilt behind the old woman's head!
She held on tight, and the heavy box dragged her backwards in an awkward dance to the door.

"O-O-Oh!"

Just as she thought she would fall and land on her caboose, the box hit the door. With a BUMP and a Boom, it bounced off the wall, sending the woman forward. Off she went in a whole new direction.

"Reowww!" squealed Folly. The old woman had stepped on his paw.

CRASH! The stepstool fell over.

Thump. Thud! Shoe boxes dropped to the floor. Sandals and clogs flew everywhere.

In the middle of it all, something in the box rattled as if broken. Then from inside came a scary *Hee hee hee! Hee hee hee!*

Wisdom ran and hid behind a curtain.

With another sudden jolt, the commotion ended. The box was wedged on a shoe shelf.

Everything stopped.
All went silent.
No one breathed.

Wisdom was worried and afraid to look. Folly had done it again! Oh, why can't he just learn to use reason?

The old woman caught her breath and steadied herself. She checked to see if she was alright. Was anything broken? No, no broken legs, no cracked elbows, no fractured hip.

"Whew," she sighed.

Wisdom was relieved that the woman was O.K.

He was just about to hiss at Folly to show his disapproval, when the lid to the box burst wide open. A toy Halloween witch popped out, cackling even louder than before.

Hee hee hee! Hee hee hee! Hee hee hee!

Both cats ran under the bed. The old woman grabbed her heart and let out a gasp!

"Gracious me!" she said.

Then all of a sudden, she began to laugh. She laughed at the silliness of it all. She laughed so hard that she had to roll on the floor.

"Well, my kitties! We've started this Halloween season off with a bang, haven't we?" said the old woman.

"A bang, and a thump!" she added when she caught her breath.

That tickled her even more, and she laughed harder still.

"And a cackle, too! A witch's cackle! . . . Oh, what a hoot."

The old woman loved her own jokes very much.

Wisdom was happy that all was good, but he knew that the Halloween season was full of adventure and fun, and sometimes, mischief and mishap. Wizzy hoped that Folly would be more careful, because you just never know what will happen on All Hallows Eve!

When the laughing was finished and the woman got up from the floor, she noticed Folly's limp. She tried to put a bandage on his foot, but Folly would have no part of that. His paw was only a little sore. He's been limping mostly for attention.

Wisdom was not pleased with Folly. He had tried to tell him, as always, to be careful and to keep a safe distance. Why on earth the woman was so forgiving, he couldn't imagine. They were lucky to be loved so much.

Nevertheless, Wisdom decided, it was important for Folly to understand that Halloween is a special time. There was much to teach young Folly about proper Halloween etiquette and responsibilities for cats.

"We can risk no mishaps that might interfere with a healthy and happy Halloween," he reasoned.

Part 2—Mystical Cats

While the old woman straightened the mess, Wisdom took Folly aside.

"There are some things you should know," he began.

"It is very natural, Folly, for cats like us to get thrilled and excited around Halloween. It's our time. Cat time! We have an extra dose of energy this time of year.

"But—and, I can't emphasize this enough, Little Buddy—we have to control ourselves. We must be extra cautious and channel our energy toward Halloween responsibilities. It is more important than you yet know."

Folly was intrigued. He knew the world felt special just now. Somehow the atmosphere was different of late. Sort of magickal and wonderful.

Why, just the other day, he could have sworn he saw the old woman fly out the window on a broom! It must have been a dream.

But Folly was too young to remember another Halloween. What was it all about? Why was it special for cats?

Wisdom explained, "Halloween is a time when cats are at their very best. They are at their most magickal, most intuitive, most beautiful. We feel like we have swallowed the moon! No one knows for sure just why this is. But one thing is for sure: Cats are THE most important animals for Halloween."

"Oh, sure," he went on, "The bats, the owls, the spiders? They think they're hot stuff around Halloween. And they show up at costume stores and on party invitations. Some even get their own movies. Even rats!

"But the cat . . . The Noble Cat . . . is the true Halloween totem. It is WE who embody the glories of this holiday!"

Folly listened. He felt pride growing in his chest. Or was that just a throbbing from when a shoe fell on him earlier?

"Witches are the queens of Halloween," Wisdom continued. "And it is cats who are the favorites of all true witches! It is cats who witches know best and love the most. It is we who are their best friends, their most trusted companions, their wisest consorts. It is CATS who understand the mysteries of Halloween."

Wisdom was on a roll.

"Why, just look at the woman, our woman," he suggested. "Is it a spider that she talks to when she's knitting? Is it a bat that keeps her company in the garden? Do owls help her decorate for parties? You tell me! Is it a rat that sleeps on her toes when she's cold?"

Before Folly could answer, Wisdom exclaimed, "No!"

Folly jumped.

"It's us! You and me, Folls! The way I see it, at Halloween, our woman is the witch around here, and we are her trusted Familiars. We have important responsibilities! It is up to us to make sure Halloween goes well!"

Folly was interested more than ever. He had never realized.

Wisdom continued. He told Folly that he would share a few stories about some Halloween cats of olden times. Learning about his ancestors would help Folly understand his role as a Halloween kitty. Folly needed to learn from the ones who had gone before, from those whose legacy carried the wisdom— Oh, the *WISDOM*—of Halloween.

"Why, Wizzy! You are really worked up. I've never seen you so, so . . . " Folly searched for the right word.

"So proud? So spirited? So regal?" Wisdom suggested.

"Well, I was going to say *wordy*. You know, like when someone talks too much."

"I'll ignore that," said Wisdom.

"Now, let me tell you about my great-uncle Midnight. Now that was a Halloween cat! Uncle Midnight was a solid black cat. Big. Strong. A real tomcat. A king among cats! Midnight's hair was like black satin—silky and shimmering. Why, it was so shiny that it actually reflected the moonlight."

Wisdom lowered his voice to a whisper. "It was said that under the light of a full moon, you could see your own reflection in his fur. Just like looking into a mirror. Some say, that if you looked long enough, especially under a Halloween moon, you could see your future in the reflection—You know, like if you'll get fat when you are old, if you'll meet a pretty female and have kittens. That sort of thing.

"Rumor had it that some of the most important people would come to his house and ask his person to let them look at their reflection in Midnight. They hoped to see the future and to learn what they should do with their lives. His person usually laughed at the requests and sent them away with candy for a treat.

"But there was one exception—and I have this on good authority. One Halloween when there was a bright full moon, Midnight was sprawled out on the kitchen table, nibbling on a tuna sandwich (he was very spoiled), when a party guest peaked at Midnight's fur.

"This person was a small boy at the time. He didn't know what he wanted to do when he grew up. But when the boy looked at Midnight's shiny belly, and smelled the tuna on the cat's breath, he began to see a vision. This vision so inspired the boy that he knew what he was supposed to do with his life. He was destined to do one of the most important jobs in all the world! He was to become more important than the mayor, the preacher, or even the school teacher."

Folly could hardly contain himself. "What did he do? What did the boy become? Who could be more important than a mayor or preacher or teacher?"

"Well," Wisdom continued. "That boy grew up to become a fisherman and started his own cat food business. You see that face on the canned food we eat every day—Mr. Whiskers the Tuna Man? Well, that's him! Mr. Whiskers was that little boy! And, you and I owe our superb canned dinners to Mr. Whiskers and the hope and vision that Midnight gave to him on that very auspicious Halloween night!

"No! Really?" Folly had never thought that Mr. Whiskers was a real person. He wanted to know more about Midnight.

"Well, Folls, I'll tell you. Uncle Middy once told me a great secret. I'll share it with you: All the best Halloween cats are black. Mysterious, velvety black. That's the mark of a true witch's cat, he said."

Wizzy had more to tell.

"Then there was my grandmother, Blanca" he continued. "A pure white beauty. A grand dame of the finest feline traditions. Turkish Angora, she was. Royalty.

"Oh, such grace! Such poise! She would glide across a room so gracefully, with her thick, long hair floating about her that it looked as though she were walking in a cloud.

"In fact, it almost looked as if she herself were floating. More than one human said that Blanca must have been a spirit cat, a ghostly apparition."

Folly shivered.

"And charm!" Wisdom continued. "Oh, how she could work a room. She would waltz into a parlor full of humans, slink onto a silk cushion, and ignore them all.

"But they couldn't ignore her. Oh no!
     They would ooh-and-aah at her beauty.

"One by one, as if under a spell, each person would be compelled to pet Blanca. One after another would set down his teacup and leave his cushioned chair to pay homage to the queenly cat. Everyone wanted to touch her gorgeous white coat and gaze into her sparkling green eyes. Even allergic people. It was as if they were under the spell of her beauty.

"Each time someone petted her, she purred a lovely song that made them smile. She had a way of making everyone feel as if they were filled with a warm light."

"Now, Folly," Wizzy confided, "the thing about Blanca is that she never meowed—Well, almost never."

Folly was shocked by this. "What? Why? How did she beg to go outside?"

"Well, Blanca was such a happy cat that she simply purred everything. She purred when she wanted food, she purred when she wanted to be petted, she purred when she was asleep. Her person knew which purring sound meant one thing or another.

"But once a year, Blanca meowed. Only once! And, that one time was on Halloween night.

"You see, Folly, each Halloween, Blanca's person was a witch. She would wear a tall pointed hat of purple velvet with black feathers. She dressed in a green cloak and carried candy to Trick-or-Treaters in a black cauldron.

"Each year she prepared a very special Witch's Favorite Treat, a special prize given to only one very lucky child. Sometimes the prize was a giant bar of chocolate. Sometimes it was a huge orange-and-white lollipop. One year it was a plastic pumpkin filled with cookies.

"But it was always very special, and the children believed that the witch's magick treat would bring them good luck all year."

"But who got the special treat? How did she choose?" Folly wanted to know.

"Well! That's where Blanca comes in. The witch determined that the child with the scariest costume would win the treat. She declared that Blanca would be the judge.

"So, every year, the neighborhood children worked very hard to create their scariest costumes. Competition was stiff, because Blanca was not easily frightened.

"One after another, the children would knock at the door and say "Trick or Treat!" The witch and her ghostly kitty would greet them, eager to see the creative costumes.

"Usually, Blanca would just stand at her witch's feet and purr.

"But once—and only once—every Halloween, one of the children was so scary that Blanca would yell out a horrified, "Meeeeee Owwww!" and run under the sofa.

"That was the signal that she had chosen the scariest costume. Whoever could make Blanca meow on Halloween was the winner!

Folly was fascinated. What kinds of costumes frightened Blanca? Who were the esteemed winners?

Wisdom told him that the mystery of how Blanca chose the winner was just that, a mystery. It came to her by some special

Halloween intuition that only Blanca understood. One year she might choose a ghost, another year it might be a vampire or even a princess.

One year she saw a—*Well, it is just too scary to say what she saw*—but she didn't come out from under the sofa for the rest of the night!

"Folly, Blanca shared her most magickal secret with me. She said that all the best Halloween cats are white! Spirit-white. White cats have the moon inside them, she said."

"But, Wizzy, you said that black is the best . . ."

"Don't interrupt, Folly. Wait until I've told you about Pumpkin. Not a very dignified name, I'll grant you.

"But Pumpkin embodied one of the most important aspects of Halloween. And, you really should know about him.

"Yes. Pumpkin the Tabby. Pumpkin the Great."

At that moment, the woman interrupted Wisdom's story. She came bouncing through the room with Halloween decorations in her hand and singing a silly Halloween song. It went like this:

Orange and fat
Round and bald
Pumpkins are the best of all!

"Oh, that's weird!" mewed Folly. "It is as if she knew you were talking about Pumpkin!"

"Yes. Eerie, isn't it?" Wisdom nodded solemnly. "But that's the kind of thing that happens around here at Halloween."

Folly wanted to know more about Pumpkin.

Wisdom told him about the legendary orange tabby, who it was said was the very essence of Halloween. Pumpkin's original name was Spindly, Spindly the Young. Spindly was a skinny kitten, always too busy to eat. Sometimes he ate too fast and would get sick at his tummy. Spindly's family worried about his health.

"Sound like anybody you know, Folly?"

"Hey! I eat slower now. I'm getting to be a big cat, don't you know?"

"Yes, and so did Spindly. As he got older, he discovered how much he liked to eat. And, he ate a lot. He liked all the usual stuff—tuna, chicken, liver. And, cream. Oh, he loved the cream. Why, you should have seen him at that ice cream social back in . . . well, anyway.

"Eventually his people quit calling him Spindly and dubbed him Pumpkin the Great, because that's what he looked like: a great big pumpkin.

"The name was extra good for him because he was such a perfect Halloween cat. Pumpkin supervised all of his family's Halloween activities.

"He liked the kitchen stuff the best. He would linger at his woman-person's feet while she made candy, brewed hot cider, or rolled out Halloween cookies.

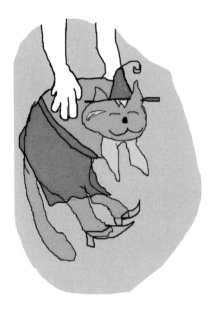

"Pumpkin helped his man-person hang spooky decorations.

"He watched over the children as they put on their costumes and helped them sort through their candy bags after Trick-or-Treating.

"He was a real family man, that one. Oh, how he loved to play with his children! He let them dress him up in silly Halloween costumes. They would put tiny witch hats on his head or tie bat wings to his collar. One year they even put a ballerina's tutu around his fat tummy.

"But Pumpkin didn't mind. He always played along and did funny tricks to match his costume. The family filled a whole scrapbook with pictures of Pumpkin in those crazy outfits. On the front of that book they wrote:

Pumpkin the Great—Our Halloween Cat.

"What made Pumpkin so special? Well, this is what he told me. Pumpkin said that in order to be a natural Halloween cat, you had to be orange. Orange is the color of fall, of squash, falling leaves, and, of course, pumpkins."

Folly was getting frustrated. Was it black? White? Or orange?

But what did it matter anyway? He wasn't like any of those cats. Folly began to look sort of sad. He wondered if he had any hope at all of being a good Halloween cat.

Then Wisdom said, "You know Folly. Pumpkin knew another secret about Halloween. One that is even more important than being orange. All those things that he did for his family made them happy. He kept them laughing and having fun."

"You see, Folls, Pumpkin understood that being a Halloween cat carried only one real responsibility—Love. No matter what jobs a Halloween cat has to do, no matter what special talents it might have, all of its magick comes from Love."

Then Wisdom said, "My Halloween talent is—and yes, I do have one—my talent is passing on the knowledge, *the wisdom*, of our noble ancestors. This is to help you live a wiser life. I am your mentor. Your big brother. That's why I feel special."

"But what about me, Wizzy? I don't have anything special."

"What? Nothing special about you? Folly, I think you are just about the most special cat I know!"

"Yeah? Really?"

"Just think about it. How many cats have survived the rocking chair and come out with such a fun-looking crooked tail?"

"My tail looks fun? I have a fun tail?" Folly was amazed.

"Of course, Silly. Don't you see how the humans laugh every time you point it at them? It is like a magickal wand that shoots laughter! That's a pretty big deal, I'd say."

"Wow. My tail as a magickal wand. Like a cat wizard."

"And just look at all the trouble you get into."

"Yeah, I know." Folly looked a little dejected.

"What I mean is this: You get into all kinds of fiascos, and yet you always come out O.K. Nobody ever stays mad at you for long. Nobody has ever been injured too seriously. It's like you are charmed.

No matter how much you mess up, things always turn out alright. I've never seen anything like it. There has to be a supernatural reason. Goodness knows, I can't figure out any other explanation."

"Me, charmed? It seemed more like I was cursed. Destined to cause trouble."

Folly tilted his head in thought. The throbbing in his chest was easing up. Why, that high heel in the closet could have killed him! But it didn't. Interesting.

"Charmed! I am charmed!" Folly meowed and purred all at once. He jumped high in the air—without watching where he might land.

"Well, I wouldn't rely on that too much," Wizzy cautioned. "You never know when a charm can go stale. I still say it wouldn't hurt to be a little more careful."

Folly nodded wisely. Wizzy decided to add one more thing.

"You know, Folly. The most amazing thing is: Our woman loves you. After all the fiascos, all the messes, all the times when she's taken a tumble because of you, she still thinks you are very fine. She tells you so every day."

Folly tucked his head and lowered his eyes. He really had caused a lot of foolish problems. He was sorry for that.

"What's more . . ." Wisdom continued.

There was more? Wizzy was certainly in a talkative mood. Was he going to be like this all the way to Halloween?

"After all that," Wizzy said, "the woman thinks you are wonderful. She forgives you no matter how big the mess or how narrow the escape. She really loves you. And, like I was saying earlier—Halloween cats are masters at Love. Apparently, you are a Natural!"

Folly was humbled. He was amazed to hear Wizzy giving such high praise. Folly decided that he owed it to their woman and to Wizzy to do something extra special for Halloween.

He would find a way to say thank you for all the forgiveness. Folly wanted to show Wizzy that he had listened to his advice.

Yes! He would earn the title of "Halloween Kitty."

By the time Halloween finally arrived, everything was decorated. There were ghosts floating in the trees, glowing jack-o-lanterns guarding the front steps. And battery operated bats flew across the front door whenever Barney the postman tried to deliver the mail.

The front porch was a little too scary for Wizzy. But not for Folly. One day he chased the electric bats and landed on Barney's shoes. His claws got stuck on the shoe strings, and he flounced about in the most ridiculous way.

Barney laughed and helped Folly get free. He told the old woman that his grandson Jimmy talked about Folly and Wisdom all the time.

"He really likes those cats of yours!"

Inside the house, the woman hung three brooms from a ceiling fan. She decorated each with sparkly ribbons of silver, purple, and orange. Then she tied a witch doll to each broom.

When she turned on the fan, the witches flew magickally through the air, ribbons of light streaking behind. The woman ran the fan whenever friends came to visit, to everyone's delight. Folly made the attraction even more fun by chasing the brooms and trying to catch the ribbons.

Wisdom enjoyed watching, but he did so from under a table—in case one of the brooms came flying off and landed on his head.

The woman was in a very festive mood. She wore a different witch's hat every day. On Monday she wore a black hat, on Tuesday an orange hat. Wednesday she showed up with a bright pink hat, with mounds of yellow and blue feathers around the rim.

"If I'm going to be a witch, I'm going to be a pretty one," she said. "Besides, Wednesdays can be rather dull. We need some color to pick us up!"

Thursday was another surprise. She pinned a tiny, green velvet hat high on her head. That's because Thursday was baking day. She needed something small and practical that wouldn't get in the way.

For Halloween she baked cookies with chocolate and cookies with pecans. She made popcorn balls and candied apples. She made something all green and gooey, too. Monster Mash, she called it. The cats weren't sure how—or why—anyone would eat it. But it made the woman laugh as she scooped it into little bowls to save in the freezer.

The woman laughed a great deal—especially when she saw herself in the mirror wearing one of those wild hats.

She sang more than usual, too. By the time Halloween came, she had sung every spooky song she could remember.

Wisdom found himself purring along with the tunes and bobbing his head to her songs about purple creatures that ate people, witchy women, and werewolves who lived in England.

Wisdom smiled as he watched Folly dance alongside the old woman, both of them jamming to the golden oldies, as the woman called them.

Off and on, all week long, little Jimmy came over to visit. He helped with the decorating. He tasted the cookie dough. He learned all the words to the Halloween songs.

The cats and Jimmy had great fun. The woman told them all stories about ghosts she had seen. This kept everyone just a little nervous. But that's how they liked it at Halloween.

Jimmy wanted the woman to read his tea leaves and foretell his future. But he changed his mind when she told him that he would have to drink a cup of hot tea without any sweetener. Jimmy was a little boy, and he didn't much care for hot tea, let alone without honey or sugar.

The woman told Jimmy that she had something better for him, something more suited for a boy his age. The woman went to a special drawer and pulled out a Halloween gift.

"This is a very special hat," she said.

She handed him a red toboggan with green stripes. It just fit Jimmy's head.

The hat was very warm and quite handsome, but the colors seemed more appropriate for Christmas. The woman explained that this hat was a magickal hat.

If at midnight on Halloween night, Jimmy put it on his head and slept in it all night, something wonderful would happen. It would happen sometime between that night and Christmas. He would be blessed with something very special.

"Like what?" he wanted to know.

The cats were curious, too.

"I'm not sure exactly," she said. "But at the very least, your head won't get cold."

Together they all giggled.

"They say that this hat will bring you the blessing that you most need," the woman said. "And, they say, you will have enough of that blessing to share."

"Well, if that comes true, I'll share my extra stuff with you."

Everyone wondered about what kind of blessing the hat might bring.

Jimmy said all he wanted was to always have a nice friend like the woman and to have cats to play with all the time.

Of course, this was all pretend, right?
No one really believed . . .

Part 4—Folly's Talent

The old woman's Halloween party was planned for late that night, for after Trick-or-Treating. The woman wanted to make sure she had time to enjoy the children in their costumes. She made cute little treat bags for each child and filled them with store-bought, pre-wrapped candy. She prepared a special basket to hold the treat bags.

Shortly before sundown, the woman pulled her rocking chair onto the porch. It was heavy, to be sure, so Jimmy helped. The woman dressed in her most elaborate witch's hat and robe. Her gray hair stuck out in all directions. She wore red-and-white striped stockings and a pair of funny looking boots.

"I'm not about to wear those pointy shoes with high heels anymore. I'd fall for sure!"

Jimmy said her boots looked even more witchy than the pointed shoes. She sat in the rocker, with the treat basket in her lap and waited for the children to come. Jimmy turned on some spooky sounds. He switched on a machine that made smoke come out of a cauldron, which was extra scary.

The boy decided that it would be more fun to help pass out candy than to go Trick-or-Treating himself. The woman was pleased. The cats were thrilled.

"The cats have to stay inside, of course," said the woman.

Folly was disappointed. He had hoped to help pass out candy.

Wisdom consoled him and explained all the reasons that it was best for cats to be inside when humans are running around in the dark.

"Talk about dangerous! You don't want another kink in your tail from that rocker, or to have some little hobgoblin step on your paw! It is best to stay inside."

So it was settled. No one would listen to Folly's protests. He was doomed to remain indoors on Halloween.

He sulked for a while, lying near the door. Maybe there was some way he could get out to join the fun. How else could he be a real Halloween cat?

"Here come some children!" Folly heard Jimmy say.

But Folly couldn't see. He wanted to look out.

"Folly, all you have to do is look out the window," Wisdom said. "And, don't worry. There will be a party later on . . . "

As soon as Folly heard the word *window*, he leaped to get a look. Just as he landed on the window sill and looked through the glass, he saw a child wearing a werewolf mask. It was staring him right in the eye! Why, that wolf face was only inches on the opposite side of the glass.

"Reowwwwww," he screeched.
His tail went up!
His back arched!
His hair stood on end!
What's more . . . the lights from the porch hit his eyes and made them glow red!

"Augggggggghhhhhh!" The child fled in terror.

As he ran down the street, they all heard him say, "Beware! Beware! That lady is a real witch. I know. I saw her scary cat!"

Everyone laughed, even the children.
The woman laughed until tears came from her eyes.
Jimmy laughed so hard his side began to ache.
But it was Wisdom who laughed hardest of all.

"Folly!" he said, "You have discovered your Halloween talent!"

It was true.
Now Folly understood his special Halloween gift.

For the rest of the evening, Folly would crouch quietly under the window, waiting patiently for another child to stand close to the glass.

Wisdom was his lookout. He watched secretly from a distant window and gave Folly instructions.

"A little ghost is getting close. Nope. The ghost left. But here comes a clown. Get ready! Wait . . . wait . . . almost there. Now, Folly! Now!"

Folly would leap suddenly to the window ledge. He would arch his back, flatten his ears, fluff his fur, and . . . *this is the best part* . . . he held his head at just the right angle to catch the light and make his eyes glow red.

"Reowwwwww!" His screech was horrifying.

There would be screams, the sounds of feet running and candy spilling on the ground.

Then came the laughter. Lots of laughter.

Everyone wanted one good scare on Halloween night. And Folly was the one to give it to them!

"I'm so proud of you, Folly!" said Wisdom. "You really are a special cat! Who knew you had such talent?"

Part 5—Magick Is Real

The woman and the boy agreed that they had the best Trick-or-Treat time ever!

Eventually it grew late, and Jimmy went home. The woman got ready for her party.

"I hope Jimmy remembers to wear his magickal toboggan tonight," the cats heard her say to herself.

The grown-ups' party was wonderful. The woman bragged on her cats and showed them off. She told everyone about their magnificent team work.

The guests had a great time. They stayed late and ate all the Monster Mash.

The next morning the woman was tired. She hoped to sleep in. But she and the cats were awakened very early to a loud knocking at the door.

It was Jimmy. He was wearing his red and green hat and talking very fast.

"You won't believe it! A cat came to my house this morning. She sneaked in through the garage door. And, we get to keep her! Mom says we have to take care of her because she will have kittens soon!"

"Oh, that's wonderful," the old woman said.

"Yes!" said Jimmy. "She is really beautiful. She has long white hair and green eyes! She is so pretty that you just have to pet her. And she purrs all the time!"

Folly and Wisdom both looked at each other.

No way! they thought.

"I wanted to name her Whitey, but my mom said Blanca is a better name for a girl. It means the same thing. Got to go! We're going to buy a litter box! And cat food!"

Off he ran, thrilled beyond measure.

"No! It can't all be!" Folly mewed in Wisdom's ear. "Can it?"

Wisdom just shook his head in wonder. He didn't know what to say. Was it the same Blanca?

The old woman went to the kitchen for her morning cup of tea. As she walked away, the cats heard her giggle and say to herself,
"Nobody ever believes me about that hat!
Of course, it doesn't usually work that quickly."

Christmas Mystery

On very cold days, Wisdom and Folly cuddled together. They lay at the hearth and enjoyed the warmth from the fire.

The old woman wore fuzzy socks that she'd knitted, a big black sweater, and a yellow one, too.
By the fire she sat, rocking and knitting.

Just every now and then, the woman stopped rocking to sip hot cocoa and look out the window.

"The snow is so pretty, and the day is wonderfully quiet," thought the woman.

"And just look at my sweet kitties, all curled up at my feet! How grand is this? Just me and my cats, all safe and sound, all happy and warm."

She stood up from her chair and went to a table. There she found a music box. It played all kinds of songs, with old-fashioned bells and chimes.

Some songs were for holidays, some for dancing. She switched on the box and turned the knobs just so, until she found some songs that were just right for this snowy day.

The music was nice, a sweet melody of bells.

When Wisdom heard it, he opened one eye. Folly raised his head and meowed to say thank you. Then both went back to sleep, purring just a little louder.

"Oh, how happy I am," thought the old woman.

As if he heard her, Folly meowed in his sleep.

The old woman began to think. Christmas was just around the corner. It might be time to get out the ornaments, stockings, and other things she had stored away.

"Perhaps after lunch, when I've finished knitting."

And so went the morning, like many before. The cozy threesome basking in love.

But on this particular cold and snowy day, something happened to throw a little excitement their way.

You see, just about then the doorbell rang. Wondering who it could be, the woman put down her yarn and went to the door. Who stood there but . . . ? *No one*. No one was there.

"Now who could have rung that bell?" mumbled the old woman. "I know I heard it. I'm not senile."

She went back to sit in her chair. A few minutes passed and the doorbell rang again.

"They must have come back."

The old woman got up once more and opened the door. Again, no one was there.

"Humph," she frowned and wondered what to make of it.

On the way back to her chair, the woman bent down and petted her cats. They purred a hello and stretched a bit.

"This getting up and down is hard on my knees when the weather is cold like this," she said and slowly went back to her chair.

She had no more than sat down when the bell rang again.

"Why that is three times now. Someone better be there!"

This time she sneaked up to the window and peaked out before opening the door.

"What was going on?" she wondered.

Wisdom and Folly were curious now. They followed behind her, all slinky and cautious.

Even Folly was careful with this strange occurrence. He still remembered her ghost stories from Halloween.

The woman was startled to see a shadow. A tiny person was running away. It looked like a child of four or five, maybe six or seven.

Then she saw what he had done. That little person had left something at the door.

He'd rung the bell three times to get her attention! But she had never looked downward to see the package.

The old woman opened the door once more. This time she saw what she had not seen before.

MEoW-Y ChriStmaS

CATNIP TEA

There on the stoop was a rather large basket. A note lay on top. It read:

Dear Madam,

I know you like cats.

Wisdom and Folly are lucky fellows to live with you.

Here are some little gifts to make you all happy. I can't think of a better place for these things to be.

Please enjoy, and make them a part of your warm happy family.

Happy Holidays!

A Secret Santa

P.S. PLEASE OPEN RIGHT AWAY!

A surprise. A mystery. Oh, how fun!

The old woman bent over, looking around for clues. She lifted the basket into the room, Wisdom and Folly close at her feet.

"My, my. What have we here? Do you see that, Sweeties? Someone's brought us a holiday gift."

The basket held several bags. One for Folly, one for Wisdom, one for the old woman. And, there was also one very strange bag that wasn't marked at all.

"Well, my pets, we are to open these right away, says the letter."

She handed Wisdom his package.

Cats love sacks because they make noise. Wisdom pawed slowly at the bag and swatted cautiously at the curly ribbon.

"This is a fun toy," he thought.

But Wisdom was wise and cautious, as always. He was a bit slow to look inside. One shouldn't be too trusting of gifts from strangers, you know.

The old woman decided to help Wizzy.

"It's all right, Sweetie. I think it is fine."

She pried open the top and showed Wisdom what was inside.

It was a fuzzy, pink mouse toy with a bell on its tail! How marvelous!

Wisdom was eager to play with his new toy. He wanted to pop it right in his mouth! Instead he sniffed and pawed and watched it awhile. He let the woman make sure it was safe. Then off he went, tossing it high.

"What a great gift! I've always wanted a mouse toy!"

Now, Folly thought all this caution silly. He tore open his bag in a jiffy! The ribbon was fun, and the bag was great. But what was inside was really cool! A rubber lizard! Woo hoo!

Off he went, tossing the lizard high in the air, flipping and flopping, rolling and pawing. Lizards are just the most wonderful toys.

Wisdom smiled at Folly. "Maybe this rubbery, reptilian toy will keep the real outdoor lizards safe," he thought. Folly was forever terrorizing the garden lizards. More than one poor little fellow had had to regrow a tail!

Folly jumped. He leaped. This lizard was great. It didn't run away! And its tail didn't come off just because you pounced on it! Folly was so happy with his new toy that he leaped too high and knocked over a lamp.

The old woman opened her bag. Inside she found a lovely jar of catnip tea. The woman was thrilled. She loved herbal teas, and catnip was her favorite. She knew just how to brew it with honey so that it tasted best.

But what was in that other strange bag, the one with no name?

"Come here, kitties," she said. "Let's look inside."

They all gathered around. The bag was not small, it was a pretty good size.

Wisdom decided that the gift must be something that could be shared with everyone. Maybe a bottle of milk. Even the woman liked milk. Yes, some nice, rich milk would be just the thing.

Folly thought it must be a special trap for catching lizards! Why, what could be better? He thought they should tear open the bag right away.

"Oh, Folly," sighed Wizzy. "What is it with you hunting lizards?"

Just about then, the bag wiggled—just a little.
    They all jumped back.

"Did you see that?" said the old woman.

It wiggled again.

Wisdom crept backwards and watched with care.

Folly jumped with joy and meowed really loud.
"It's a real live lizard! I knew it! I knew it!

A great big iguana!"

The old woman put her hand in front of Folly and cautioned him to go slow.

The bag moved again. There was indeed something inside. It was trying to get out.

"Maybe it is a robot toy that moves on its own," Wisdom suggested.

Folly hoped it was a lizard robot.

The bag started to wiggle hard and shook violently about, making all kinds of sack noise. The old woman's eyes grew wide and her back went straight.

Wizzy tucked his head low and pulled in his tail.

Folly jumped onto the rocking chair seat, which started it swaying back and forth. He had barely caught his balance when the bag suddenly stopped moving.

Everyone moved their chins forward a bit. No one made a sound. No one moved.

Wisdom decided he should be the brave one of the three.

He sneaked slowly forward, his ears flattened and his tail low to the ground.

Very, very cautiously, Wizzy lifted his paw to touch the bag.

Suddenly, a strange, tiny sound came from the bag.

Wisdom stepped back. "Did you all hear that?"

Folly jumped from the chair and stood by Wisdom. He put his nose to the sack when . . . the sound came again. It was a very soft mewing noise, like a little elf cat.

Confused, Folly and Wisdom looked at one another.

"OH!" said the woman. "I recognize that sound!"

Quickly, she opened the bag. And, just as she suspected, there inside, was a very tiny kitten!

"That's no lizard!" mewed Folly.

The woman lifted the furry baby to her arms.
"How adorable! How sweet! Look fellows, another tiny mouth to feed!"

Folly thought, "I am not sharing my lizard toy."

Wisdom thought, "I hope this fellow listens better than Folly does."

Then Wizzy and Folly came closer to see. What a cutie it was, they both agreed. All furry and soft, with big blue eyes.

Someone had stuck a little red bow on its head and tied a note around its neck.

The note read:

Hello, New Family.
I don't yet have a name. Please give me one.

"So, what shall we call the newbie?" Folly meowed. "I think Lizzie would be best. Or, if it's a boy, Lizzardo!"

As if the woman had almost understood Folly's meowed suggestion, she looked the little kitten in the eyes and said, "Hello, little Newbie. Welcome home. Welcome to your new family."

Life would change for everyone now. The woman began to plan what all had to be done. She would have to knit a new Christmas stocking with the name Newbie on it. She would need to get a special little dinner plate for the kitten and a basket for sleeping.

The woman smiled and held the baby cat close to her heart.

"Well, you've had a big day, Little One," she whispered in a soft motherly voice. "But you look healthy. Someone has taken good care of you. What soft fur and a sweet little tummy. Everything seems intact. Nothing's broken or hurt."

Then the woman saw the lamp that had fallen. She sighed and then laughed. "Well, at least nothing important!"

"Oh, Folly," she said, "you'll have to be more careful with a baby in the house. Broken lamps can be dangerous."

At that, Folly and Wisdom both jumped onto the woman's lap, where they purred softly and put Baby Newbie to sleep. It was a little crowded in that rocking chair, but no one cared.

The old woman had never been happier.

"Why, what could be better" she thought, "than three loving cats curled up in my lap?"

Out on the porch, a little boy peeked in the window and smiled. He wore a red toboggan with green stripes.

"She'll never know that I am the secret friend who brought the Christmas surprise," thought Jimmy.

The old woman said one last thing before they all fell asleep: "I'll have to remember to *not let Jimmy know* that I know he is the Secret Santa who gave me a kitten.

What a sweet boy!"

About the Author

Tales of Wisdom & Folly is Dr. Blum's first fictional series, which she says is "just for fun!"

She lives in Houston with her husband Bill, and their fluffy baby, Maisie. When Francelle and Bill adopted Maisie as an eight-week-old kitten, Maisie immediately cast a spell over the Blum household, happily changing their lives forever. She has since become a loving companion and gardening buddy. She is the artistic inspiration and writing muse behind this series. Were it not for Maisie, *Wisdom & Folly* might never have come to life.

Wisdom & Folly offers adults and young readers the chance to revel in the everyday antics and adventure of two very special cats and their very forgiving and delightfully eccentric old woman. Whether you want a little adventure or just need some laugh-out-loud time, let yourself fall into the special world that Wisdom and Folly call home. You'll want to stay there!

Dr. Blum hopes her readers will have as much fun with these stories as she has had in creating the characters and their little world, where mishap and mayhem go hand-in-hand with forgiveness and love.

We hope you enjoy Book One of this series.

For more information on Francelle, Maisie, and *Wisdom & Folly*, go to **TalesofWisdomandFolly.com**. You can also follow us on **Facebook**.

Tales of Wisdom & Folly™

Book Two

By Francelle Blum

Coming Soon!

talesofwisdomandfolly.com